Published in the United States 1995
by Dutton Children's Books,
a division of Penguin Books USA Inc.
375 Hudson Street, New York, New York 10014

Library of Congress Cataloging-in-Publication Data
Mahurin, Tim.
Jeremy Kooloo/by Tim Mahurin.—1st ed.
p. cm.
Summary: One word for each letter of the alphabet tells
the simple story about the antics of A Big Cat.
ISBN 0-525-45203-6
[1. Cats—Fiction.   2. Alphabet.]   I. Title
PZ7.M27725Je   1995
[E]—dc 20   94-20462
CIP   AC

Designed by Sara Reynolds
Printed in Hong Kong
First Edition
1 3 5 7 9 10 8 6 4 2

A Big Cat

Drank

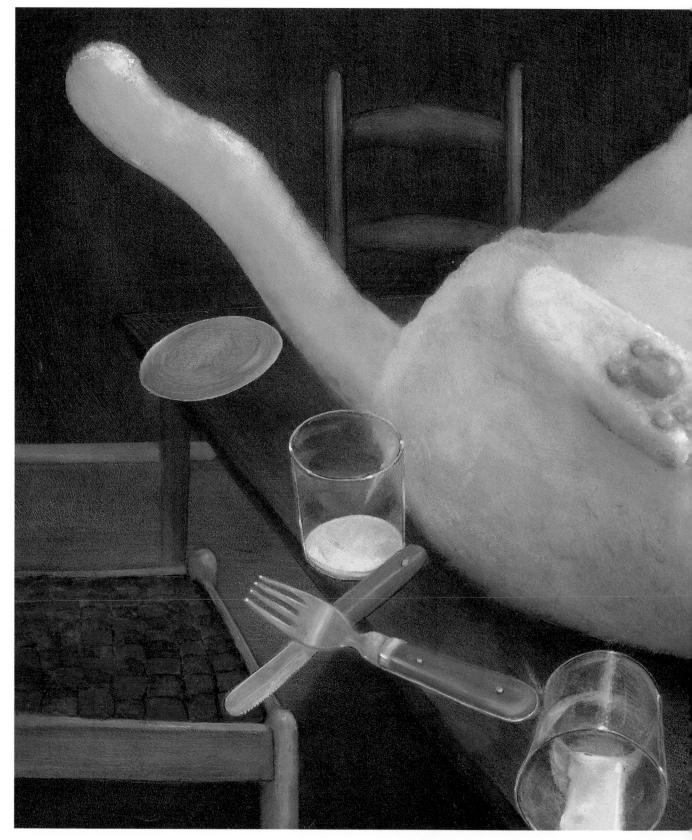

Full Glass.

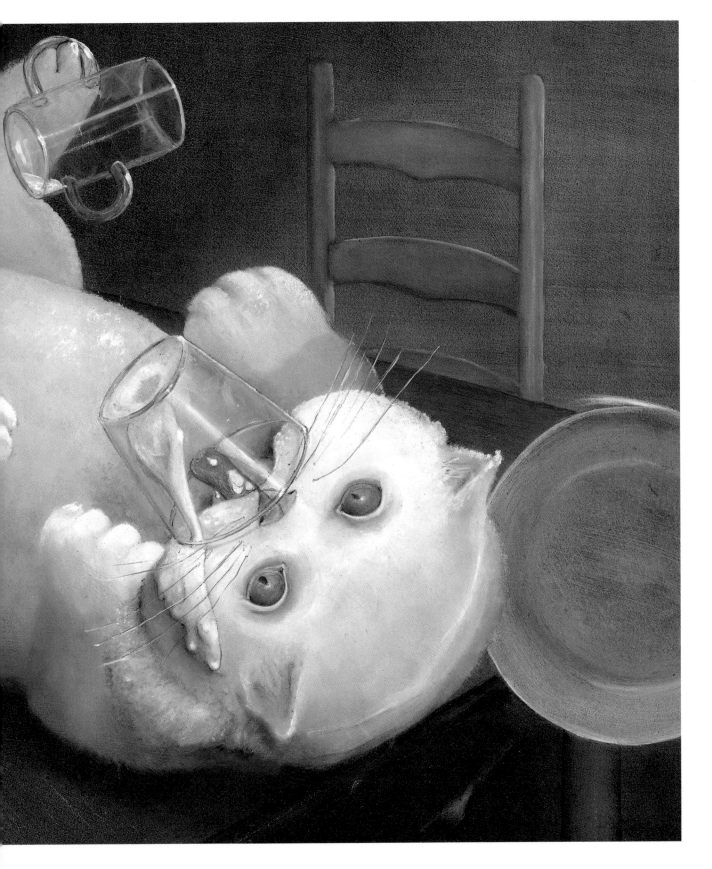

Hiccup!

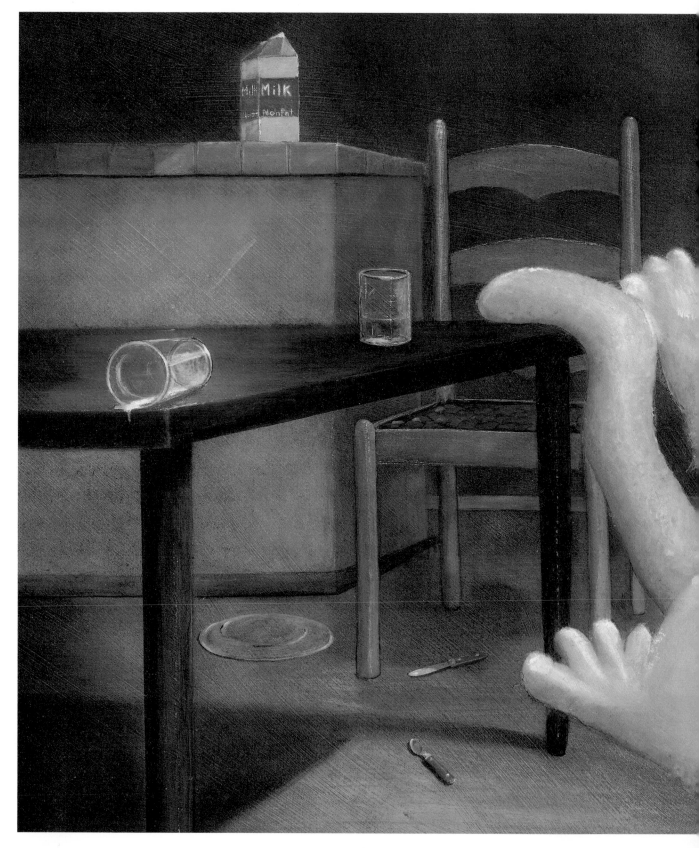

Indeed,

Jeremy Kooloo

Loves Milk.

Nonfat

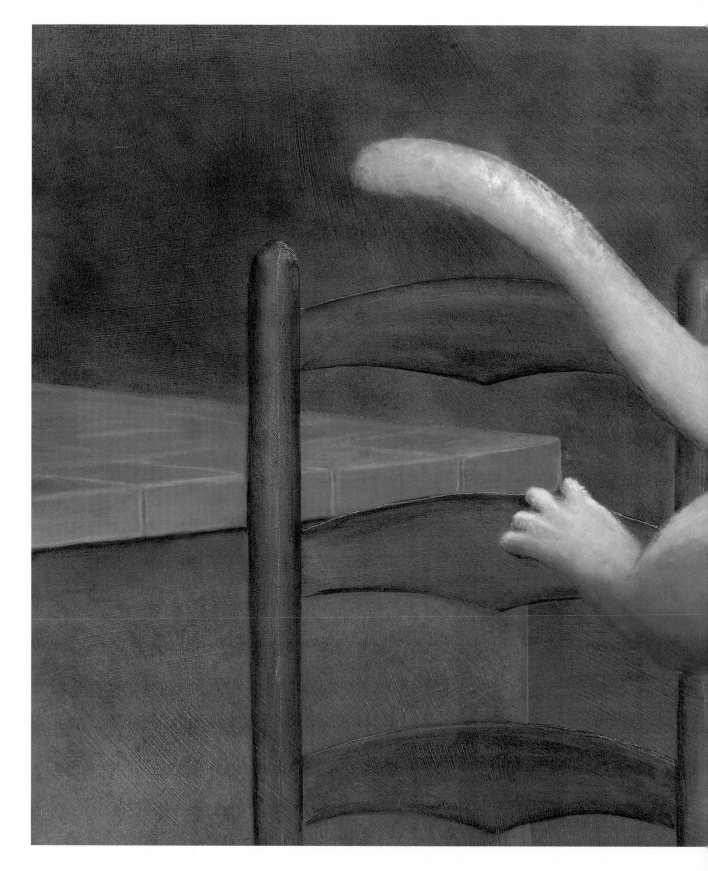

Oops!

Quick, Run.

Stretch . . .

Tired

Under Very

Warm XYZzzz

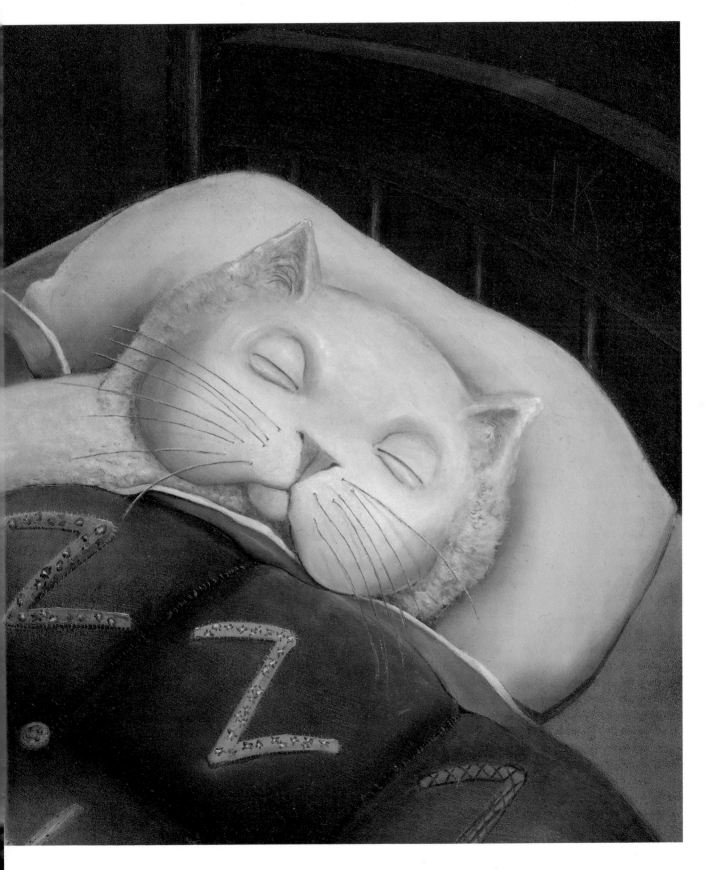

A
Big
Cat
Drank
Every
Full
Glass
Hiccup
Indeed
Jeremy
Kooloo
Loves
Milk
Nonfat
Oops
Prrrrrrr
Quick
Run
Stretch
Tired
Under
Very
Warm
X
Y
Zzzz